The Selfish Princess

ISBN 978-1-64258-894-1 (paperback)
ISBN 978-1-64492-913-1 (hardcover)
ISBN 978-1-64258-895-8 (digital)

Christian Faith Publishing, Inc.
832 Park Avenue
Meadville, PA 16335
www.christianfaithpublishing.com

Printed in the United States of America

The Selfish Princess

Gina Manfredi

Once upon a time, King Phillip and Queen Isabella lived in a beautiful castle. They had a daughter. Her name was Stella. The little princess was beautiful, but she was also very spoiled.

The king and queen gave her everything she wanted. However, Princess Stella did not like to share. She never let any of the other children in the kingdom play with her toys.

One day, when she was playing in the garden with her dolls, another little girl who was just her age came up to her.

"What's your name?" the stranger asked.

"Stella," replied the princess.

"I'm Aria," said the little girl.

"Your dolls are very pretty."

"Thank you," replied Stella.

"Can I use one so we can play together?" asked Aria.

"No, they're mine," answered Stella.

"That's not very nice," Aria told her.

"I don't care," replied Stella angrily. "They are my dolls, and I do not have to share them with anyone."

Stella picked up her dolls, ready to leave the garden. Suddenly, Aria was transformed into a beautiful fairy.

Stella was amazed. Aria waved her hands over the dolls. Suddenly, they were turned into blocks of ice. Stella began to cry. She dropped the ice blocks.

"That's not very nice!" she screamed. "Change them back!"

"No," said Aria. "Until you can learn to share your toys, they will remain in these ice blocks."

Stella went back to the castle. She was surprised to see that all of the toys in her room had been put in blocks of ice too. She cried and cried.

Her parents bought her some new toys,

but they too were turned to ice. For the next few weeks, Stella stayed in her room. She sat at her window and watched the other children in the kingdom playing and having fun. She turned from her window and sadly looked around her room and all the blocks of ice.

She went outside to where the children were playing, but no one asked her to join the game. She went back to the garden. There was a little girl there, sitting and making chains out of the many different kinds of flowers. She was dressed in a dress that was way too big for her.

"What are you doing?" asked Stella.

"Making pretty necklaces," the little girl answered.

"Why aren't you playing ball with the other children?" asked Stella.

"They will not let me play," replied the little girl.

"Why didn't you bring your toys to play with?" asked Stella. The little girl looked very sad.

"I do not have any toys," she replied.

"Why not?" asked Stella.

"There was a big horrible storm in our village. Our house was destroyed and all of my toys were broken."

Stella looked sad too. "Why can't your mommy and daddy get you new toys?" asked Stella.

"My mommy and daddy had to go away to find us a new place to live," explained the little girl. "So now I live with my grandma. She is really old and does not have any toys at her house."

She looked at Stella and asked, "Do you have toys?"

"Yes. Maybe we can play with them later," said Stella, not wanting to tell the girl what happened to her toys.

"Can you show me how to make a necklace?"

"Sure," replied the little girl

"My name is Violet."

"I'm Stella," said the princess.

"Do you live in the castle?" asked Violet.

"Yes, I do," answered Stella.

"Wow!" said Violet.

The two girls sat there, making flower chains. After a while, the queen came out to the garden.

"Stella, it's time for lunch," said the queen.

Stella looked at Violet. "Can she come too?" asked Stella.

"Who is she?" asked the queen.

"Her name is Violet," replied Stella. "She has no toys because they were broken in a storm. Her mommy and daddy went away."

"Of course," said Queen Isabella.

As the two girls followed the queen to the castle, Stella heard a noise behind them and turned to see what it was. Aria was standing there, smiling at her. Laying at Aria's feet were Stella's dolls now unfrozen.

About the Author

Gina is originally from Northeast Ohio. She graduated with a bachelor of arts degree from John Carroll University in 1995. In 2000, she moved to Naples, Florida. She has enjoyed writing stories all her life. She enjoys teaching young children who are the inspiration for this story. She is very active in many ministries involving young people at her local church. She enjoys spending time with her family. He favorite vacation spot is Walt Disney World.

CPSIA information can be obtained
at www.ICGtesting.com
Printed in the USA
BVHW062308101219
566271BV00002B/3/P

9 781644 929131